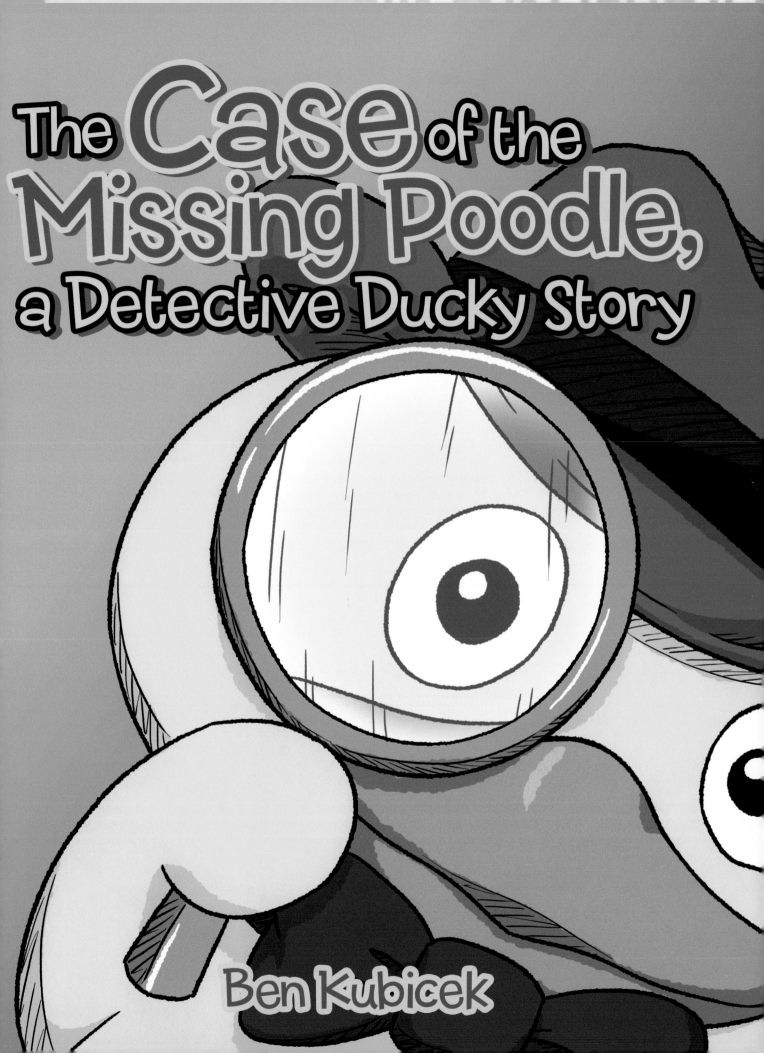

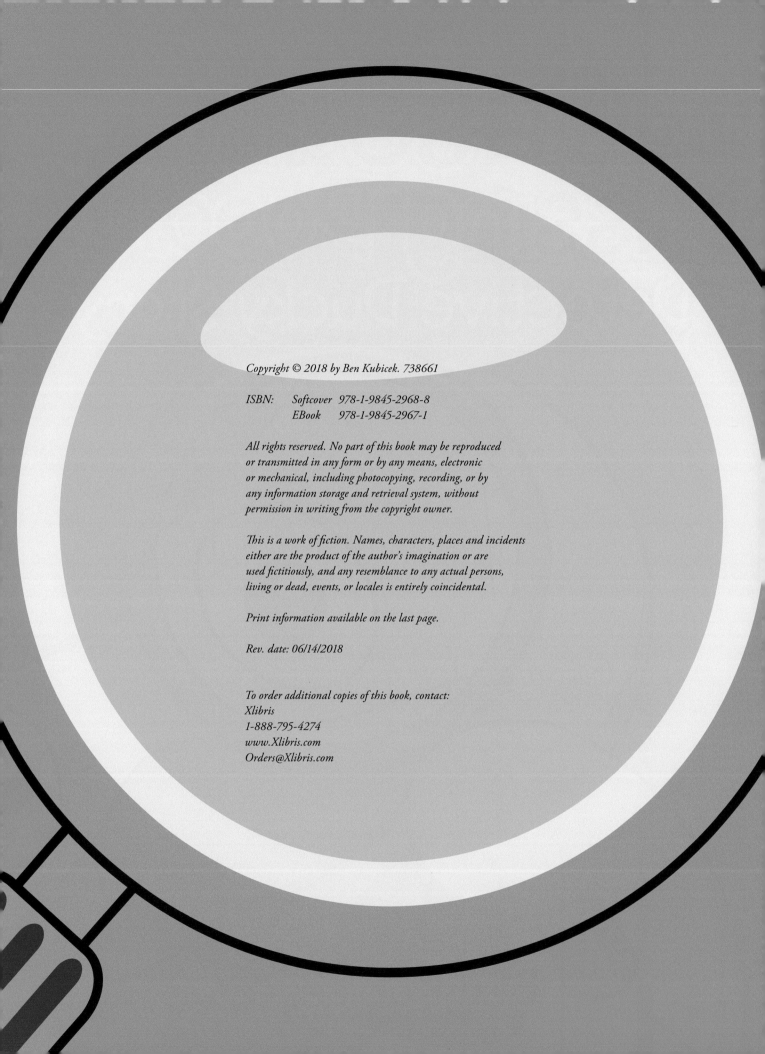

To order additional copies of this book, contact:
Xlibris
1-888-795-4274
www.Xlibris.com
Orders@Xlibris.com

The Case of the Missing Poodle,
a Detective Ducky Story

I want to thank Erik Stone for creating the concept art.

It was a cold dark night. Aren't all detective stories supposed to start that way? Ok, it wasn't really cold or dark, it was about 11:30am and sunny out. Anyway, my name is Ducky, but when I put on my detective hat I become Detective Ducky. I was sitting in my office, about to eat a plate of beans, waiting for my next case. If only my legs were longer, I could lean back in my chair and put my feet up on my desk.

All of a sudden, my office door swung open and a distraught looking young lady walked in. I guess my beans would have to wait. I hoped I could fix whatever her problem might be. I didn't like seeing her so sad and upset. She must have been about 13. Her long blonde hair was wet from tears. She could really use a Kleenex.

"Hi my name is Betsy, I have heard you help people find things," she said through watery blue eyes.

"You heard correctly," I responded, as I handed her a box of Kleenex. "I charge $20 a day plus expenses."

I asked her what she wanted me to find. She said she had lost her pet poodle named Poopsey. I thought to myself, if my name was Poopsey I would want to get lost too. She looked like she was about to cry again when I told her I would help her find her dog.

I was on the case. The first stop was to see the last place her poopy dog, I mean Poopsey, had been seen: the dog park. We arrived at the local dog park after a short walk from my office. It was like what you would expect; A large fenced in area, where you can take your dog off the leash and let them run around and play. I noticed this park had a lot of trees and bushes.

Betsy said that two hours ago she came here with her poodle. She sat down to read a book while her dog played. I found that interesting. Most of the time, dogs want to play with their owners at the dog park. After about a half an hour, Betsy called for Poopsey, but she never came. Betsy looked everywhere, but could not find her missing poodle.

I decided I should check the dog park for evidence. I wondered if this could be a kidnapping case. Perhaps Poopsey was some rare breed of Poodle that was worth a lot of money. I didn't see any drag marks on the ground. You would expect to see some, if a dog was dognapped out of the park. I decided to go and check out the bushes.

Now I have to admit, being a duck that looks a lot like a chew toy in a dog park is not the most comfortable feeling. I remember being a small young duck and being afraid of big dogs. Most dogs would love to treat me like a toy to play with. Thankfully, I can handle myself. I was the world duck wrestling champion two years in a row. One of my favorite things to do is wrestle someone to the ground and yell 1, 2, 3, I win!

A large German shepherd came over to see if I might be something fun to chew on. I told him this wasn't a duck he wanted to mess with. I hoped he didn't see the bead of sweat falling from my brow. He was more than twice my size. He didn't heed my warning, so I quickly put him in his place. My wrestling training kicked in and he was pinned to the ground in two seconds flat.

You should have heard the squealing that came out of that dog. I am not sure if it was the dog's squealing or my yelling 1, 2, 3, I win, but after that the other dogs gave me plenty of room as I looked for clues.

I finally ended up at a large bush in the corner of the dog park. It seemed like you could just slip under some branches. I pushed my way through and found myself eye to eye with a downcast looking poodle. I said, "Hello, my name is Ducky. I am looking for a lost poodle. Are you lost?"

The poodle said, "I don't want to say my name. It's embarrassing."

I guess I found our missing dog. "Is that why you won't come when your owner calls for you?" I asked.

"Yes", she said, "I don't want anyone to know my name."

"I might be able to help you with that," I responded. "What if Betsy gave you a new name?" Poopsey had hope in her eyes when she told me the new name she wanted. I crawled out of the bush and found Betsy.

I told Betsy I found her missing poodle and that she wanted a new name. What was Betsy thinking naming her dog Poopsey? I whispered the new name in Betsy's ear. Betsy called out, "Princess, Princess, it is time to go." At once Poopsey, now called Princess, came out from under the bush and came running to Betsy.

Betsy thanked me for my services and paid me my fee. It was a happy reunion between owner and poodle. There were wet slobbery kisses everywhere. I was glad everything ended well and I was twenty bucks richer. It just goes to show, you should be careful what you name your pets. As for me, it was time to celebrate closing a case with a nice plate of beans. Did I mention I like beans? They are my favorite.

Printed in the United States
By Bookmasters